Julia Emote

LET'S TALK ABOUT KINDNESS AND GRATITUDE

THIS BOOK BELONGS TO

....

....

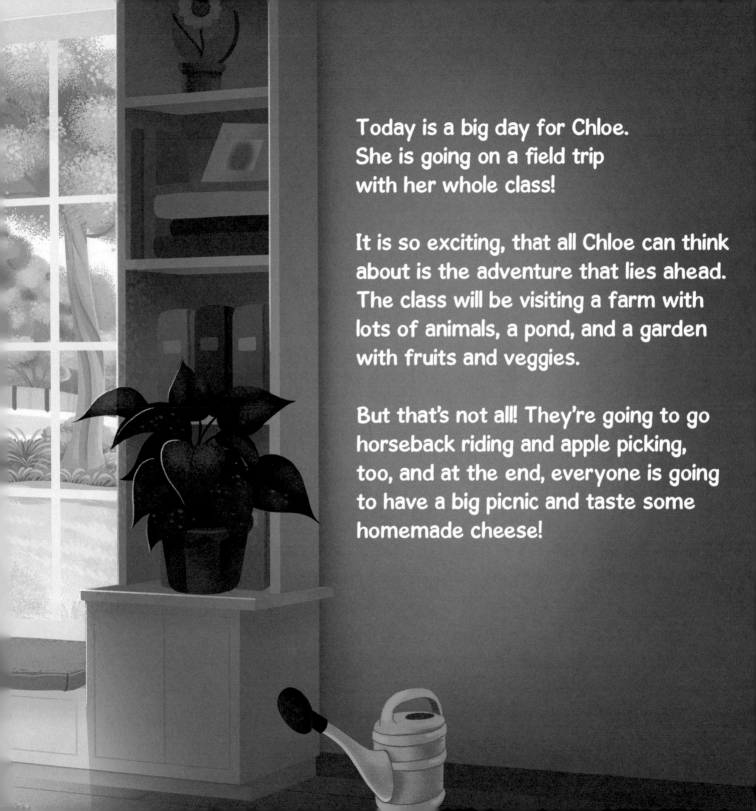

Today is a big day for Chloe.
She is going on a field trip
with her whole class!

It is so exciting, that all Chloe can think
about is the adventure that lies ahead.
The class will be visiting a farm with
lots of animals, a pond, and a garden
with fruits and veggies.

But that's not all! They're going to go
horseback riding and apple picking,
too, and at the end, everyone is going
to have a big picnic and taste some
homemade cheese!

Uh oh, bad news! Chloe's favorite travel toy, Foxy, is missing. She looks everywhere: in the washing machine, next to the cookie cupboard in the kitchen, by the living room window, and under the stairs — she cannot find him!

To make things worse, Chloe's best friend Charlie
doesn't feel so well today; he has to stay home.
All of this has Chloe feeling grumpy and sad.

Mom brings Chloe to the bus and kisses her goodbye.
"It's so great that you're going on this adventure today.
Your teachers must have worked really hard to organize it.
Make sure you say thanks to them, okay, Chloe?"

On the bus, Chloe forgets to say hello to Dean, the bus driver.

She finds a seat next to Ms. Rice,
a kind and cheerful teacher,
who is also Charlie's mom.

Ms. Rice is pleased to see Chloe.
"Chloe! Charlie asked me to give this to you.
He is working on making kindness an everyday habit."
Then she hands Chloe a shiny yellow boomerang!

"The best things in life are from the heart, and they always come back, just like this boomerang will come back to you in the park."
"How can I be more kind?" asks Chloe.

"There are so many ways you can be kind. It is not always easy, but kindness will always make someone's day better.
Let's look for examples right around you!
Smile, say hello, or tell someone that they look good today —
you don't even need to know a person to show them kindness!

Today, I want you to watch your classmates during our trip and notice all the acts of kindness, big and small, that they perform."

Chloe and her class arrive at the farm.
She starts watching her friends to spot
their acts of kindness.
She sees Brian let Melinda go for a horseback ride first.

She sees that Thea made a sketch of the farmer
on her tippy toes picking fruit for the kids,
and now Thea is giving it to her as a present.

Frank brings a confused
little yellow duckling back to its mom.
The others build a bird feeder together.

After farming, the class is allowed to pick apples and take them home!
Lucy helps little Jane pick fruit off the trees and feed the horses.
Joe has dropped his apples in the lake, so Angela gives him half of hers.

Surprise! The entire class is having a picnic to enjoy some homemade cheese and fresh bread, along with delicious fruits and lemonade made from those fruits.

The kids have had a wonderful time and are feeling grateful. And guess what? The trusty yellow boomerang is right there to help them express it. Let's spread gratitude by saying, "I'm grateful" to everyone that made us happy today!

Back home, Mom gives Chloe her Foxy toy that she found near the window. Chloe shares her memories of the day's trip with Mom. "My class spread lots of kindness today!" But what's that?

"Beep beep!" Sounds like Dad's car.

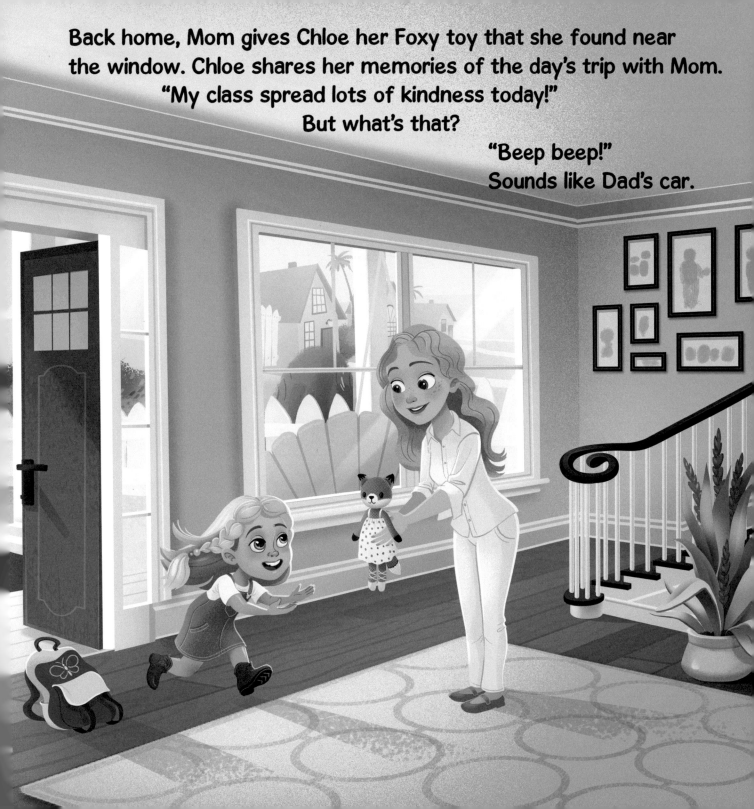

Dad has brought home a new dog
from the shelter. A new member of the family!
A thankful, happy, wagging tail!

"This day is worth being thankful for, isn't it? We should always notice good things happening around us and be grateful for them."

The next day, Mom and Chloe get busy baking yummy apple pies with the apples they got from the farm. One of them is for someone special.

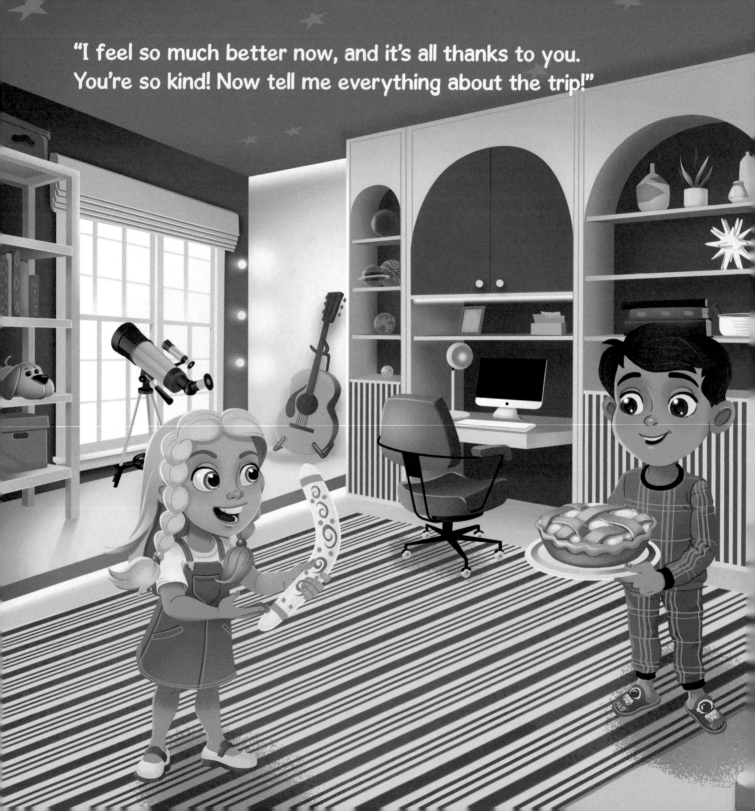

"I feel so much better now, and it's all thanks to you. You're so kind! Now tell me everything about the trip!"

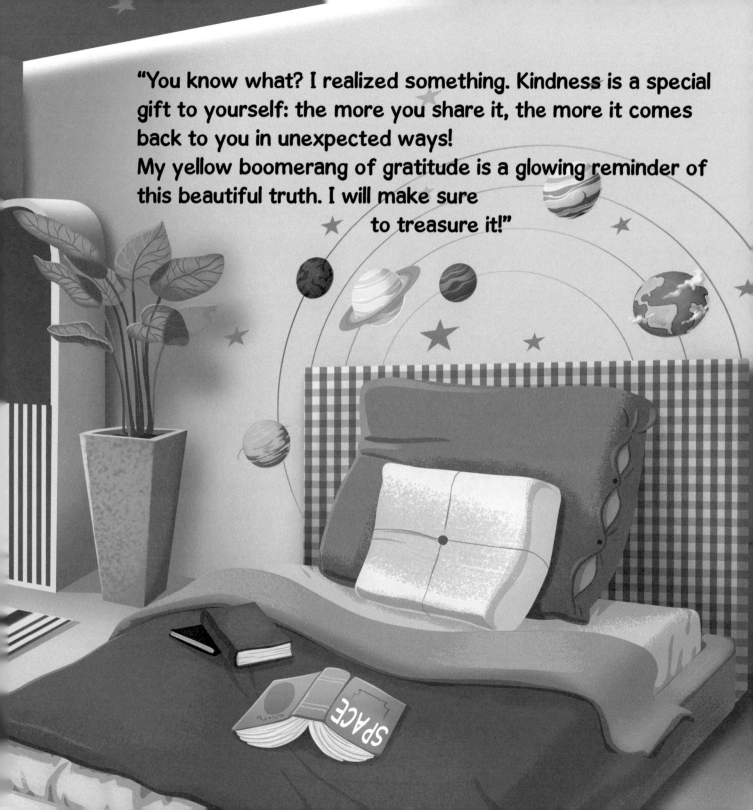

"You know what? I realized something. Kindness is a special gift to yourself: the more you share it, the more it comes back to you in unexpected ways!
My yellow boomerang of gratitude is a glowing reminder of this beautiful truth. I will make sure to treasure it!"

LET`S TALK WITH CHLOE:

1. What does it mean to be kind?

2. How can you show kindness to your friends or family?

3. Can you think of a time when someone was kind to you?

4. How does it feel when someone is kind to you?

5. Who are those people you would like to say "thank you" to, and what for?

In a world where Chloe skips and plays, a QR code hides a kindness maze. Scan it quick and go ahead, life with Thank you's is just great!

Your review is important to us!

Hello, my dear Reader! I am thrilled you've joined us on our second journey in the "Let's Talk" series. As Chloe's tale of kindness concludes, I hope it has left a warm imprint on your heart. If it has, please extend that warmth by sharing a review. Your insights nurture the spirit of gratitude and guide others to the kindness that lies within our stories.

Beyond the pages, I welcome your thoughts and ideas, and even your hellos. Connect with me at juliaemote.com or drop a line at julia.emote.author@gmail.com. Your engagement is the very essence of the boomerang of joy that, once thrown, always returns.

Thank you for being a part of this journey and for sharing your valuable perspective.

If you enjoyed this book and if you find it giving you the best knowledge, please write a review of it!

With love,
Julia Emote

P.S. Your voice helps kindness circulate far and wide—may it always find its way back to you.

Let's use our imaginations, kind readers! Remember our super boomerang, Charlie's present to Chloe? It definitely needs your serious input to become an outstanding one. Come on, decorate it in the most amazing way!
Have a blast creating your own Boomerang of Kindness!!

Made in the USA
Thornton, CO
03/06/24 18:15:25

6281277a-333f-4a3b-98c9-a0891f8232c2R01